D1573211

Parents and Caregivers,

Stone Arch Readers are designed to provide enjoyable reading experiences, as well as opportunities to develop vocabulary, literacy skills, and comprehension. Here are a few ways to support your beginning reader:

- Talk with your child about the ideas addressed in the story.

- Discuss each illustration, mentioning the characters, where they are, and what they are doing.

- Read with expression, pointing to each word. You may want to read the whole story through and then revisit parts of the story to ensure that the meanings of words or phrases are understood.

- Talk about why the character did what he or she did and what your child would do in that situation.

- Help your child connect with characters and events in the story.

Remember, reading with your child should be fun, not forced. Each moment spent reading with your child is a priceless investment in his or her literacy life.

Gail Saunders-Smith, Ph.D.

Stone Arch Readers

are published by Stone Arch Books
a Capstone Imprint
1710 Roe Crest Drive
North Mankato, Minnesota 56003
www.capstonepub.com

Copyright © 2013 by Stone Arch Books

Library of Congress Cataloging-in-Publication Data
Crow, Melinda Melton.
Rocky and Daisy at the park / by Melinda Melton Crow; illustrated by Mike Brownlow.
p. cm. — (Stone Arch readers: My two dogs)
Summary: Rocky and Daisy are two dogs with too much energy and
a trip to the dog park seems like the perfect answer.
ISBN 978-1-4342-4163-4 (library binding)
ISBN 978-1-4342-6118-2 (paperback)
1. Dogs—Exercise—Juvenile fiction. 2. Parks for dogs—Juvenile fiction. [1. Dogs—Fiction.
2. Exercise—Fiction. 3. Parks—Fiction.] I. Brownlow, Michael, ill. II. Title.
PZ7.C88536Rpc 2013
813.6—dc23   2012027138

Reading Consultants:
Gail Saunders-Smith, Ph.D.
Melinda Melton Crow, M.Ed.
Laurie K. Holland, Media Specialist

Designer: Russell Griesmer

Printed in the United States of America in Stevens Point, Wisconsin.
092012
006937WZS13

Rocky and Daisy at the Park

by Melinda Melton Crow
illustrated by Mike Brownlow

MY TWO DOGS

I'm Owen, and these are Rocky and Daisy, my two dogs.

ROCKY LIKES:

- Chasing squirrels
- Playing with other dogs
- Chewing things
- Running with me when I ride my bike

DAISY LIKES:

- Playing ball
- Listening to stories
- Resting on the furniture
- Eating yummy treats

Rocky and Daisy loved to play in the backyard. Rocky chased squirrels. Daisy fetched the ball.

But there were problems.

Rocky dug holes in the yard.

Daisy always ran through the garden.

"Owen, the dogs need exercise, but they don't follow the rules," said Mom. "Can you take them on a walk instead?"

So Owen tried taking Rocky
and Daisy on walks. But there
were problems with that, too.

Rocky liked to run. Daisy did
not like her leash.

Walking them did not work.
And Mom did not want them in
the yard.

"How will Rocky and Daisy
exercise?" Owen asked Mom
and Dad.

"Maybe we should take them
to the dog park," said Dad.

"What's a dog park?" asked
Owen.

"It is a big park where dogs can run and play without a leash," said Mom. "There is a fence to keep them safe."

"Let's take Rocky and Daisy
to the dog park today!" shouted
Owen.

Everyone climbed in the van. Rocky jumped right in, but Daisy would not budge. She was so scared of the car she started shaking.

"It's okay, Daisy," said Dad.
He helped her climb in.

At the dog park, Owen took
off the leashes. Rocky stood still.

Daisy stood still, too. They didn't know what to do at a dog park!

All of the other dogs were running and jumping and digging. "Go and play," said Owen.

"Hooray!" shouted Rocky. He
ran over and sniffed all of the
dogs. Then he started running
with them.

Rocky ran too fast. He tried to stop, but he slid into a mud puddle. Yuck!

"Oh, Rocky," said Owen.

Daisy didn't want to play
with the other dogs. She hid
behind Mom. "I thought you
might be scared," said Mom.

Mom pulled Daisy's ball out
of her pocket and threw it. "Go
fetch!" she said.

"My ball!" shouted Daisy. She
ran after her ball.

Daisy brought her ball back for Mom to throw again and again. She did not like all of the dogs, but she loved playing ball.

Rocky wanted to show off for the other dogs. He grabbed Daisy's ball and buried it in the mud.

Daisy dug out her ball. Now she was muddy, too.

"Time to go home," said Dad.

This time, both dogs needed
help getting into the van. They
were tired and dirty from all their
playing.

Owen looked at his muddy dogs and grinned. "I think Rocky and Daisy had a great time," he said.

"How do you know?" asked Mom.

"You can't get that dirty without having fun!" said Owen.

THE END

STORY WORDS

exercise	budge	muddy
leash	sniffed	tired

Total Word Count: 430

READ MORE
ROCKY AND DAISY
ADVENTURES!

STONE ARCH READERS — LEVEL 3 — Rocky & Daisy Go Home

STONE ARCH READERS — LEVEL 3 — Rocky & Daisy Go Camping

STONE ARCH READERS — LEVEL 3 — Rocky & Daisy Get Trained